First American Edition 2016
Kane Miller, A Division of EDC Publishing

For information contact:
Kane Miller, A Division of EDC Publishing
P.O. Box 470663
Tulsa, OK 74147-0663
www.kanemiller.com
www.edcpub.com
www.usbornebooksandmore.com

Library of Congress Control Number: 2015954254

Printed and bound in the United States of America
3 4 5 6 7 8 9 10

ISBN: 978-1-61067-499-7

THE WARRIORS
OF
BRIN-HASK

Cerberus Jones

Kane Miller
A DIVISION OF EDC PUBLISHING

CHAPTER ONE

"So I call her Arabella Moonglow," said Sophie T., "because she's all white, see?"

Amelia bent over the baby rabbit in Sophie T.'s cupped hands. "She's so soft!" said Amelia.

"Yeah," said Sophie T., passing the rabbit to Amelia. "Here, you can hold her."

Amelia heard a groan behind her. Charlie was jiggling up and down, his face so warped by impatience that Amelia had to stop herself from laughing.

In a minute, Amelia thought. The end-of-school bell had only just rung, and there were heaps of other kids in the playground for Charlie to hang out with for five minutes.

"Amelia," Charlie muttered, "how long –"

"So," said Sophie T. loudly, as though Charlie hadn't spoken, "do you want one? Arabella is mine, obviously, but there are four other bunnies in the litter. Sophie F. is coming over this afternoon to pick hers. You could come, too."

Charlie coughed.

Amelia sighed and gave the rabbit one last pat. *All right, Charlie. I haven't forgotten you.*

But Sophie T. saw her disappointment, and snapped at him, "Is there a problem, *Charles?*"

Charlie instantly bristled with anger, but before he could open his mouth to speak, Amelia bundled the rabbit back into Sophie T.'s arms and babbled brightly, "Oh, my goodness, thanks for reminding me, Charlie. Sorry, Sophie, I've just remembered I have to get back to the hotel this afternoon as soon as I can ..."

She rattled on, trying to fill in the space so that nobody else could get a word in. The last thing she needed right now was for Charlie and Sophie T. to start on each other.

Sophie T. slitted her eyes at Charlie, a look of pure venom, but then turned back to Amelia and said sweetly, "Oh, don't worry about it. You can come to my house some other day. *Any* day, actually. I'm sure it would make a nice change for you not to be forced to hang out with ..." She paused, flashed a split-second sneer at Charlie, and then went on, "I mean, hang out at such a creepy old hotel."

Amelia felt a prickle of unease. She was suddenly aware that every kid left in the playground had stopped whatever they were doing, and were now listening to their conversation.

"Forced!" Charlie barked. "As if anyone would have to be forced to hang out at the hotel!"

"As if anyone asked you!" Sophie T. shot back.

"I don't need to be asked," Charlie was almost yelling now. "I practically live there! You're just jealous because no one has asked *you*."

Amelia froze. How could he say that! He knew how nearly impossible it was for Amelia to invite any of her school friends back to the hotel. She'd already been for three afternoons at Sophie T.'s,

 4

and spent one Saturday morning at Sophie F.'s, and felt really, really slack about not returning the favor. *Soon,* her mum promised. *Soon, but not quite yet ...*

And Charlie was using it against Sophie T., as though Amelia didn't want to be a real friend to her.

Luckily, by this stage Sophie T. was so angry she didn't pause to take up the point with Amelia. She just lashed back at Charlie, "Jealous? How ridiculous are you, *Charles?* The only reason I haven't been to the hotel is, I don't want to! And not just because you *practically live there*, either. Although it does prove my point, because any place you think is cool must be pathetic."

"Ha!" shouted Charlie. "Ha! That shows what you know! For your information, the hotel is –"

Amelia yelped and leapt between them, and heard herself shrieking, "Charlie! That's enough! Shut it!"

Sophie T. swelled with triumph, and turned smoothly to Amelia. "Anyway, as I was saying, before I was so rudely interrupted –"

"I'm sorry, Sophie," Amelia butted in gently. "But Charlie's right. I've got to get back to the hotel now."

She didn't look back as she and Charlie walked past every other kid in the playground and out through the school gates. Then again, she didn't need to. She could feel Sophie T.'s furious eyes on her back the whole way.

It wasn't the best start to the weekend. It was bad enough worrying about whether Sophie T. would still be her friend by Monday, and trying to sort out in her own head exactly how angry she should be with Charlie, but she also had to deal with *Charlie* being angry. And not just angry at Sophie

T. – he was angry at Amelia!

"Me?" she said. "What did I do?"

"You," Charlie said bitterly, "took *her* side and told me to shut it!"

"You were about to blurt out the whole thing! What do you think I should have done, just stood there and let you yell out to the whole school that I live in a top-secret alien hotel? That we have a gateway that connects to every known wormhole in the universe? I should have let you wreck everything just to prove I'm on *your side?*"

Charlie stopped walking and stared at her, aghast. "You think I was about to tell her *that?*"

Amelia frowned. "Yeah."

"Well, that's just insulting. *Yeah.* Thanks heaps, Amelia. That's great. You must really think I'm as dumb as Sophie T. says."

"All right, then." Amelia stood in front of him, her arms crossed. "What were you going to say?

For your information, the hotel is –" she prompted him.

"Like living on a movie set," Charlie finished. "With a real hedge maze with a fountain hidden in the middle, and an attic filled with cool junk, and an orchard with apple trees big enough to climb in. *That's* what I was going to say."

"Oh." Amelia bit her lip. "Sorry. I thought ..."

Charlie shrugged. The worst bit was, Amelia knew he was really hurt by her not trusting him.

"I get it," he said. "Don't worry. Everyone in Forgotten Bay thinks I'm an idiot. I'm used to it."

"I don't think you're an idiot! I just thought Sophie T. had made you so mad that –"

Charlie snorted. "*She's* the idiot!" He made a face and said in a high voice, "Do you have a problem, *Charles?*"

"Yeah, that was horrible."

"No, that was the funniest bit," Charlie grinned.

"She thinks she's so great, but she doesn't even know – my name's not Charles."

"It isn't?"

Charlie laughed. "Of course not. It's Karolos. Karolos Vasilis Andreas Floros." It rolled off his tongue impressively. "So now you know my secret. And believe me, if I had to choose between news getting out at school about the aliens or my full Greek name, I know which one would be easier to live with."

A kind of peace settled between them. They continued walking along the beach road towards the hotel. As they passed the shops, Charlie said, "You got the money?"

Amelia pulled out her wallet and nodded. "This is going to be ... weird."

They went into Archie's Grocery and came out again with twelve jars of mayonnaise loaded into four cloth bags. A bag in each hand, they began the slow, steep journey up to the headland.

Amelia's hands and shoulders ached from the weight before they were even halfway up.

"Surely Tom could have just driven here and gotten it himself?" Charlie grumbled.

"He said he was too busy working out what time the warriors of Brin-Hask would arrive."

"What kind of warriors eat mayonnaise? And why couldn't they come and get their own?"

Amelia snorted. "They're the guests, Charlie. We can't get the guests to do the hotel work. Plus, in case you've forgotten, aliens aren't supposed to leave the hotel grounds."

"Yeah, I don't get *that* either. I mean, you come all the way across space to Earth, and you don't even get to go surfing? What's that about?"

"Oh, I don't know," Amelia was sarcastic. "Maintaining the whole *top-secret* bit about aliens existing or something, maybe."

"But they're all wearing holo-emitters! What difference would it make? We have human guests at the hotel, and they never know the difference."

"Just how it is," Amelia said simply. "Rules of the gateway. Anyway, what if one of the holo-emitters failed? You know how freaked out we were when we saw Miss Ardman turn into a berserk dinosaur right in front of us."

Charlie nodded, and both of them shuddered.

He shook himself, and said, "Talking of failed holo-emitters, I've got bad news and, well, bad news."

"Go on."

"I still can't figure out how to get mine to shift from menu mode to cloaking mode. And also ... I sort of can't find it."

"*What?!*"

"Yeah, I was looking for it this morning, and it wasn't in my room, so then I thought I'd left it in my desk at school –"

"You took our holo-emitter to *school?*"

"But it wasn't there either. So now I don't know where it could be."

"And you're just mentioning this now?"

"I don't think I lost it at school," Charlie said calmly. "It's probably at the hotel. Hey, watch it!" he yelled as a car drove too close beside them. "Oh, it's Mum!"

They sped up, groaning as the mayonnaise jars banged against their legs, but eager to get to Mary's car.

"What on earth are you two carrying?" Mary leaned out her window, amused.

"Mayonnaise," said Amelia.

"For Tom," said Charlie, heaving his bags into the trunk of the car, and then gratefully climbing into the backseat.

"Tom?" The amusement was gone, and Mary

looked sharply at them both. "You're running Tom's errands for him?"

"We don't mind," said Amelia.

"I do," said Charlie. "Those bags weighed a ton."

Mary turned back to the steering wheel, muttering to herself.

It was a relief to sit back and let the car do all the work up the steepest part of the hillside to the hotel, which stood right at the top of the headland, sheer cliffs falling away on all sides.

"Come on," said Mary. "Leave Tom's stuff where it is, he can wait. Come inside and I'll get you a popsicle each."

That sounded perfect. Amelia followed Mary into the hotel with nothing more complicated in her mind than whether she should have raspberry or lemon. But when Mary opened the front door, there was Amelia's mum – the phone in her hand

13

and a shocked look on her face.

"It was them," said Mum. "The complaint went through, and they've decided to follow it up in person. Immediately."

The complaint? It took Amelia a second or two to figure out what Mum meant, and then she was just as stunned. Miss Ardman – their first alien guest. What a disaster that had been. So bad that Miss Ardman had threatened to report them all. And now, apparently, she had.

James, Amelia's older brother, slouched through the front door and stared at them all suspiciously.

"What's going on?"

Mum glanced awkwardly at Mary, and then said, "Oh ... a bit of bother with the Health Department. They're sending an inspector tomorrow."

Amelia frowned, not following the story now.

Miss Ardman had called the Health Department?

"On a Saturday?" said James.

The sound of falling saucepans and breaking glass exploded from the kitchen at the end of the hallway, along with the muffled sound of Dad yelling.

"Oh, for pity's sake," Mum moaned. "What now?"

A huge brown rat, its eyes glinting red in the afternoon sun, burst through the kitchen door and sped past them all.

CHAPTER TWO

As the rat scuttled over the toes of her shoes on its way through the lobby, Mum screamed.

Not in fear, not in disgust, not even in surprise. She screamed in frustration.

"This *can't* be happening! Rats in the kitchen? On top of everything else?"

Dad ran out of the kitchen in pursuit of the rat, but stopped when he saw everyone in the lobby.

"What do you mean *everything else?*" he asked her.

Amelia saw Mum lift her eyebrows warningly

in James's direction as she said carefully, "That customer complaint has gone through and *they* are sending someone to investigate tomorrow."

"They?" Dad yelped. "Tomorrow? But we've got rats in the kitchen!"

Mum put a hand to her forehead and breathed deeply through her nose.

"Well." Dad staggered a bit. "Right. Well. Uh ... it looks like we're in a bit of trouble."

"Great!" said James. "Shall I go upstairs and start packing now?"

"Not helping, James!" Mum snapped.

Mary swept Amelia and Charlie out towards the main doors and said, "Why don't you two go and tell Tom about the inspection tomorrow?"

"Oh, yeah. We've got to take him that mayo as well," said Charlie.

Amelia was only too glad to be out of there. She was so mad at James, she didn't want to be anywhere near him. *Such* a jerk. Just because he hated the hotel, he didn't care what happened to anyone else. As long as *he* got to go back to the city, who cared if Dad lost his job?

"Good old Mum," said Charlie, happily. "I was afraid we'd get stuck in there listening to boring arguments all afternoon. Come on, over here!"

"Where? What are you doing, Charlie?"

Instead of going to the trunk of Mary's car to get the mayonnaise, Charlie was tiptoeing along the veranda.

"I want to find where the rat went."

"Who cares where it went? As long as it's out of the kitchen."

Charlie looked at her in surprise. "Didn't you see it?"

"The rat? Of course I saw it. Don't really want to see it again."

"Didn't you notice its eyes were red?"

Amelia shrugged. "So? Lots of rats have red eyes, probably."

Charlie shook his head. "Lots of *white* rats do. Like Sophie T.'s silly Voldemort Moonsparkle or whatever."

"That was a rabbit, not a rat."

"Same thing," said Charlie. "White animals – red eyes. Even then, not always. Toby Finch's brother had a white dog with blue eyes. But brown animals? They *never* have red eyes. But this rat did."

Amelia stared at him. "Charlie, who *cares?* Maybe it had curly whiskers. Maybe it had seven toes on each foot. What difference does it make? The Health Inspector isn't going to be checking what color its eyes are, they're just going to shut us down!"

Charlie stared back, as though she were the crazy one. "Have you forgotten where we are?

The Health Inspector is going to be the least of our worries if that turns out to be an *alien* rat."

Amelia swallowed. *Oh*.

"Exactly. Now, are you going to help me look for it?"

"No."

Charlie blinked at her.

"Let's say you're right – and you probably are – that only makes it more urgent that we get down to Tom's and tell him what's happening."

"Ugh!" Charlie's shoulders slumped in defeat, and he stomped back to Amelia. "You can be so *sensible*."

They dragged the four bags of mayonnaise out of the car and trudged down the hill to Tom's place – through the thick magnolia trees, across the leaf-strewn clearing, to a little run-down shack.

Charlie didn't even knock, he just kicked the door open and yelled, "We got your mayo, and you're busted, Tom! Next time you want us to do your jobs, you'll have to pay us or I'm telling Mum."

Amelia winced. She set her bags down on the floor by Charlie's, and then saw that Tom was muttering over one of his charts and fiddling with a weird-looking clockwork machine. The cottage, as usual, was a disaster. Everything was so cluttered with old clocks, parchments, jeweler's screwdrivers, plates of toast crusts, broken toy engines, ancient books, cold cups of tea, springs and gadgets, it was amazing Tom could find anything.

Charlie looked at Amelia, puzzled. It was impossible that Tom hadn't heard them come in.

"Hey!" Charlie said.

Tom snapped up and glared at him, one eye fierce, the other hidden behind a black eye patch. "What?"

"Your mayonnaise," Charlie said deliberately.

"Like you asked."

"Right. Well, leave it there," Tom waved his hand vaguely towards the kitchen, his attention already back to the mess of paperwork on his desk.

"Uh, Tom ..." Amelia said. "Is there a problem?"

"Eh?"

"I mean," she said more firmly, "there is a problem. A big one, up at the hotel."

Now she had Tom's attention.

"Mum said Miss Ardman had made her complaint, and now the Health Inspector is coming tomorrow to follow it up. Plus, we have rats in the kitchen."

"Health Inspector?" said Tom. "But Miss Ardman wasn't complaining about the – *Oi!*" he suddenly bellowed, and Amelia saw Charlie freeze, more than halfway across the next room, and only a couple of feet away from the stone steps leading down to the gateway itself.

"Get out of there!" Tom blazed. "Get over here, *now.*"

Charlie recovered quickly from the shock of being discovered, and took another step closer to the stairs. "What's the big deal? I only want a look."

Tom stood up from his desk and limped towards Charlie. He was furious, but Amelia noticed, also very reluctant to get any closer to the gateway room than necessary.

"What's the big deal?" he said quietly, with an intensity that was chilling. "Don't you realize how dangerous the gateway is?"

"Dangerous!" said Charlie. "I told you, I only want to look. It's not like I'm going to go through."

Tom took another half step towards him.

"The gateway isn't an elevator. It's not like the door only opens when the car is there. The gateway is a living thing – a whole system of wormholes that are always moving and jostling one another for position. And as they move, the wormholes set off currents in space, so that the gateway is always active, always sighing, and heaving, and –" Tom shivered "– *sucking*. Anything can get pulled through if it's close enough to be caught in the current. And if you were sucked through without a wormhole to catch you, we'd never be able to find you, because you wouldn't have gone somewhere we could ever look. You'd have been lost in the *Nowhere*."

Amelia gripped the edge of Tom's table, as though the gateway were already tugging at her. Charlie, however, was shining in wonder.

"Cool," he said breathlessly.

Tom glared at him, and Charlie plodded reluctantly back to the front room.

"Right," Tom said gruffly. "Now off you go. I don't know what your parents want me to do about that complaint business, but it seems that the best thing is to get on with running the show as well as we can until then. And I've got both hands full trying to get organized for the next two arrival parties."

"*Two* arrivals?" said Amelia. "But Mum only told us about the Brin-Hask. Who else is coming?"

"What? Oh, slip of the tongue." Tom huffed and shuffled his charts around. "Go on, then, off you go. And tell your dad the feast must be ready for the Brin-Hask. There'll be trouble if it isn't."

The two kids picked their way out of the cottage, and back into the late afternoon sun.

"That went well," said Amelia dryly.

"I thought it went excellently," Charlie grinned.

"We didn't tell him about the red eyes, and you got in massive trouble!"

"No," Charlie corrected her. "We found out more about the gateway, *and* got Tom so annoyed he forgot to ask for the change from his mayonnaise. We scored nearly eight bucks!"

Amelia laughed, but stopped abruptly as the little house behind them vibrated so violently that the windows rattled. A low, grinding sound shook the ground. Amelia stared at Charlie, wondering what might have happened to him if he'd been at the top of the stairs while *this* was going on.

"Let's go." She grabbed Charlie by the arm and headed back up the hill to the hotel. Charlie went along placidly.

"I can't wait to see the Brin-Hask. I wonder if they're guns-and-bazooka-type warriors, or if they're more into death rays and lasers? I can't decide which would be cooler."

"I can't wait to find out who the second arrival is," said Amelia.

Charlie said, "I think Tom just made a mistake."

"So do I," Amelia agreed. "But I think the mistake was letting us know."

CHAPTER THREE

"We never should have come back to the hotel,"
Charlie grouched, dragging the garbage bag
behind him. "We should have gone straight back
to Archie's and spent all of Tom's money on candy.
Instead ..." He made a disgusted sound.

Amelia hoisted her own bag over her shoulder
and followed James into the next bedroom. She
and Charlie had been given a dustpan and brush
each, and had to sweep up all the rat poop and
chewed garbage they found while James, who
was wearing heavy leather gardening gloves,

checked all the rat traps and poison baits. So far, James definitely had the better job, because while Amelia and Charlie had found plenty of poop to sweep – and it *stank* – James hadn't found a single dead rat or sprung trap to deal with.

Dad couldn't see any sign of where the rat had come from in the kitchen, either.

"They've taken the cheese out of the traps," said James, "but left the poison baits untouched. It's almost as if they know what they're doing."

"Of course they do," said Charlie scathingly. "They're alien rats, aren't they?"

Amelia watched James closely and thought she saw a tremor in his cheek before he scoffed, "Are you still playing make-believe? Aliens! As if."

Charlie opened his mouth to retort, but Amelia shook her head. What was the point? If James refused to believe the gateway was real and thought Amelia and Charlie had made up the aliens as a game, *and* that (for some reason) all the adults including Tom had decided it would be fun to play along too ... well, you couldn't argue with a person that deliberately dumb. At least, arguing hadn't worked on him so far.

James got down on his hands and knees and peered under a bed. Another empty trap. And then, "Hey, what's this?"

He stood up and held out a familiar black cylinder with brass rings along its length. It was a holo-emitter. James was about to throw it in the box with the traps when Charlie said, "Wait! That's mine!"

James' eyes narrowed. "Yours? What's it doing up here, then?"

"I just remembered," said Charlie. "We were playing hide-and-seek the other day. That's when I dropped it!"

"Ah, well, in that case, then," James said kindly,

holding the holo-emitter out to Charlie. "You know what they say? Finders, keepers!"

He snatched back his hand and put the holo-emitter in the top pocket of his shirt.

"That's not fair!" Charlie was livid. "You don't even know what it is!"

James refused to be drawn. "I know it's mine now. And you could have found it yourself if you were doing a better job with that dustpan and brush."

Charlie looked like he wanted to hit James, but Amelia pulled him out to the corridor.

"What?" Charlie snapped.

"Let it go," said Amelia.

"No! Why should I?"

"Well, for one thing, you should've already given it back to Tom, so you can't really complain to anyone that you lost it. Plus," she spoke over Charlie's objections, "you haven't been able to figure out how to use it yet. If anyone can, it's

James. He's a genius with gadgets, and if you don't want to ask Tom for help, James is the best person to solve it, or fix it, or whatever the problem is. Also," and here she got a look in her eye, "if James *does* figure it out, he will have actual, physical proof in his own hands that the alien stuff is real. If you want revenge on him for anything, then let him deal with *that*."

Charlie calmed down. "Yeah, but still ..."

Amelia sighed. "OK, one more reason: the more you want the holo-emitter, the more you care, the more determined James will be to never, ever let you see it again. Act cool, and you *might* have a chance."

"Fine." Charlie turned to go back to poop sweeping when a movement caught his eye – something outside the big picture window at the end of the hall.

"Amelia! Quick!"

She ran to stand beside him, just in time to see a figure in a long, dark coat disappear into the hedge maze.

"Who was that?" Amelia said in a low voice.

"One of the Brin-Hask dudes, do you reckon?" Charlie sounded excited. "Come through early?"

"Or," said Amelia, "that extra arrival we're not supposed to know about."

Saturday was clear and beautiful. After a crisp morning down at the beach, splashing through the freezing water and hauling up seaweed, the sun was delicious on their legs. A light wind off the sea carried the sound of the waves far below, and rustled the trees so the bushland seemed to sway. Amelia sprawled on the grassy hillside with Charlie, and wondered how she had ever fit herself into that tiny apartment back in the city.

"So you still haven't met Lady Naomi?" Charlie asked. "And you live in the same house?"

"The same *hotel*. She has her own bathroom, and she never eats with us, so ... no. Anyway, you're here almost as much as I am. Have you seen her?"

Of course he hadn't, but he was spared admitting it as a huge, old-fashioned sedan crunched up the gravel driveway. Amelia knew nothing about cars, but even she could understand why Charlie scrambled to his feet in astonishment. It was a gorgeous, dark-green, elegant, luxurious *automobile*. They raced up to get a closer look.

Amelia wondered who would get out of a car like that. One of the foreign leaders Mum used to work with when she was a diplomat? Some billionaire who wanted to buy the hotel? A rock star who wanted to record an album here?

The driver's door opened and out stepped a tall, thin, slightly stooped man. He was wearing white cotton gloves, held a handkerchief to his nose, and peered up at the hotel with a foul expression. Amelia watched him take a briefcase from the backseat of his car, and then walk stiffly up the steps, sniffing with distaste as he rapped on the door.

Dad opened the door.

"Snavely!" he beamed. "I can't believe they sent you! How are things back at HQ?"

Mr. Snavely's mouth didn't relax as much as an inch as he stepped into the lobby. Dad, holding the door open for him, saw Amelia and Charlie standing there.

"Oh, kids, come on up," said Dad. His grin, Amelia saw, was slightly too wide. "I want you to meet Mr. Snavely."

Mr. Snavely turned and peered down his long nose at Amelia and Charlie and said, "Ah, yes – the *children*." He made it sound like children were a horrible disease he didn't want to catch. He turned to Dad. "Isn't there another one?"

"Another ..." Dad hesitated. "Oh, another kid! Yes, hold on a moment – James!" he bellowed up to the second floor.

Amelia was confused. Dad *knew* Mr. Snavely. It sounded like they might have worked together, or perhaps Dad just knew something about Mr. Snavely's office. Was he another scientist? Maybe he had an amazing brain, even if he wasn't very friendly. But Amelia didn't know any scientist with a car like Mr. Snavely's.

Mum stuck her head out of the library and saw who it was. "Oh, hello, Adrian. Let me go and get James for you, Scott."

She hurried up the stairs to the family wing of the hotel, while Amelia grew more and more puzzled. Why would her parents want Mr. Snavely to meet James? Mr. Snavely didn't look that keen to meet anyone. Maybe he was a strange uncle they'd never heard of before.

Mr. Snavely looked around him. "And the caretaker?"

"Tom," said Dad. "Yes, he's down in his cottage. We thought you'd probably like to see his setup for yourself."

Mum came back down the stairs, James trailing behind her. "Mr. Snavely, this is James. James, this is Mr. Snavely," she glanced at him, "the Health Inspector."

Ahh ... now it made sense. And a Health Inspector might be a kind of scientist, measuring temperatures, taking samples of bacteria in the kitchen, that sort of thing.

"And this is the extent of the spread?" said Mr. Snavely. "Apart from the caretaker?"

"And Charlie's mum, Mary Floros," said Dad. "Our housekeeper. I put it all in the paperwork

I sent you."

"Yes ..." Mr. Snavely opened his briefcase and took out a sheaf of papers. "This is what you sent us originally, before the placement began. But already containment has been breached. And with the first guest under your care! What I want to know is –"

"How the kitchen looks!" Dad blurted. "I know, it's the obvious place to start your inspection, isn't it!"

Dad led him down the hallway.

Mr. Snavely slunk into the kitchen.

"What a freak!" Charlie whispered to Amelia.

Mary came down the stairs from the guests' wing, an enormous laundry basket in her arms. "Oh, hello! You all here to help me with the curtains?"

"Err, no, Mary," said Mum. "Scott's just taken the Health Inspector to the kitchen."

"Oh." Mary bit her lip. "Well, I suppose ... well ... how bad can it be? We've only just opened. It was only one complaint. There can't be –"

Mary's attempt to look on the bright side was cut off by a high, warbling scream, and then a heavy clang, as though a saucepan had been thrown. It sounded a lot like Mr. Snavely had a complaint of his own.

"Oh, no," Amelia muttered. "I bet it's all that seaweed we collected this morning. We just dumped it on the counter."

But seaweed didn't explain the sound of more pots and pans being thrown, or why Dad was now shouting along with Mr. Snavely.

Amelia and Charlie ran to the door, aware of both mums calling them back, but unable to resist the noise. They *had* to know what was going on. Charlie flung open the door, and Amelia saw Mr. Snavely standing in the sink, holding his briefcase in both hands, his face utterly white.

She couldn't blame him. It seemed Dad had finally discovered where all those rats were hiding. For some reason, the Health Inspector must have been poking around those couple of loose floorboards in the corner of the kitchen, next to the oven. Amelia could see a carving knife wedged between two planks, as though about to pry one up. And next to that ...

She gulped.

Dad was standing three feet from the oven, a broom held defensively in his hands, staring at a hole in the floor. Two or three floorboards had been pushed up and out of the way, and in the cavity below, dozens of tiny red lights twinkled. No, flashed on and off. No, she realized in horror – they *blinked*. She was looking not at dozens of tiny red lights, but dozens of pairs of tiny red eyes. The space under the floor was filled with rats whose eyes glowed in the dark.

"This is outrageous!" Mr. Snavely said shrilly. "This isn't a containment breach any longer. We're talking illegal entries! Harboring! Total border security failure!"

"Adrian," Dad said through his teeth. "Not now."

"Forget about losing the hotel, Walker. I'll see you jailed for this! Jailed, you hear me?"

"You can't jail people for rats!" Charlie shouted.

Mr. Snavely was turning purple by now. "This is chaos, Walker. I knew you'd fail, but not this quickly!"

"It's just rats!" Charlie cried, which was very loyal of him, but totally untrue. Anyone could see these were anything but *just* rats.

Mr. Snavely shrieked again, and Amelia saw that the rats had begun to creep out of their nest. Six of them had inched forward, and now their

heads and shoulders were out of the hole, their front paws all resting on the edge of the floor. They were massive, hulking things, almost as big as cats, only more solid and far more threatening. Dad stared at them warily, and when he didn't move or try to push them back with his broom, the six hopped up in unison, landing in perfect formation.

They crept forward, and Amelia saw another six line up behind to take their place. And behind them, another twelve eyes glowed in the dark.

How many more rats were down there, all lined up in sixes and waiting their turn to emerge?

"OK," said Dad, very calmly and gently. "I think it's about time we casually strolled out of here. Kids, you first. Just very slowly wander back out the way you came. OK?"

But Mr. Snavely had his own idea. Without waiting for Amelia and Charlie to move, he leapt out of the sink, landing badly on the floor and twisting his ankle. He cried out in pain, and then again in terror as the rats charged at him.

Amelia screamed. Dad yelped and scrambled onto the oven. There was a blur of movement and a deafening crash as Charlie dove at the floor, bringing half a counter's worth of kitchen utensils down with him. Mr. Snavely jumped up and bolted, chased from the room by four or five beautifully disciplined rows of rats.

Amelia pressed herself up against the wall, but

Charlie whooped in triumph, standing on top of a huge steel colander he'd tipped upside down. "I got one! I got one!"

"Charlie!" Dad roared. "Get out of here! Amelia, go!"

Amelia ran from the kitchen, hooking her arm through Charlie's as she went and dragging him away from the upturned colander. They burst into the lobby where Mum, Mary and James still stood, their faces blank with shock.

"Are you ..." Mum struggled for something to say. "Are you all right?"

"Never! Never in all my –" stammered Mr. Snavely, before finally gathering himself. "You're *finished!*" He shrieked. "Do you hear me? We'll be back first thing tomorrow to – to deal with you people! This is the end, for all of you!"

CHAPTER FOUR

James was the first to react. Pale with fright, he snapped straight back into mega-jerk mode and said, "Well, fantastic. If anyone needs me, I'll be upstairs finishing off my packing."

No one stopped him going.

The lobby still echoed with the sound of the front door slamming behind Mr. Snavely. Amelia was shivering slightly, but Charlie was doing a curious sort of dance – one part leaping in celebration that he had trapped a rat under the colander, one part desperate frustration that he wasn't back in the kitchen with Amelia's dad.

Mum reached behind the reception desk and pressed the button that called Tom.

One last bang from the kitchen, and then Dad at last came through the door to the lobby.

"Out to the driveway, you all," he said wearily. "I don't want anyone near that kitchen for a while." He clapped his hand on Mum's shoulder. "What do you think, Skye? Good first impression?"

Mum smiled sadly.

"Hang on," said Charlie. "What about my rat?"

"Safe," said Dad. "I put a twenty-liter can of olive oil on top of the colander. He's going nowhere. Probably. Good reflexes, by the way."

Charlie beamed and, satisfied for now, followed them out.

"How bad will it be?" said Mary.

"I'm not sure," said Dad. "Adrian said we'd lose the hotel, and mentioned jail."

Mary gasped.

"On the other hand," Dad went on, "those rats have clearly been there a lot longer than we have, so they might take that into account."

"But what laws did we break?" said Amelia.

"Ah ..."

Mum and Dad exchanged looks, and the truth of the situation dawned on Amelia. "Mr. Snavely wasn't really a Health Inspector, was he?"

"No," said Mum. "He's with Gateway Control, the people in charge of the gateway network. It was Control that Miss Ardman sent her complaint to, and it's Control who have the power to take the hotel away from us."

"And send us to jail?" said Amelia.

"An *alien* jail?" Charlie asked, as though that would be a great treat.

"I don't think anyone will go to jail," said Dad. "Or not you kids, anyway. But Control is pretty unhappy that you guys found out about the gateway. One of our promises in coming here was that we would contain the true nature of our work to the fewest possible number of humans. In Control's opinion, that meant adults only. You kids were never meant to know."

"That was why I told you it was the Health Department coming," said Mum. "I didn't want you to act as though Mr. Snavely were anything other than an ordinary, boring government official. I thought it would be easier for you, avoid another pointless argument with James, and show Mr. Snavely that you didn't know *every*thing that goes on here."

Amelia thought about how she and Charlie crashing into the kitchen was exactly the problem Mr. Snavely had come to inspect. "Sorry."

"Don't worry, cookie," said Dad. "By the time Mr. Snavely saw those rats, there wasn't anything you could do to make things worse."

"Are they really rats?" said Amelia.

"I'm not sure," said Dad. "It was a stroke of genius Charlie caught one, though – gives us a chance to find out what we're dealing with." Charlie glowed with pride. "Ah, here's Tom."

Tom stamped up the last rise, breathing heavily and looking harried.

"I'm not sure I've gotten the calculations right," he called to Dad. "There are two different ways to work out when the wormholes will align, but I'm getting different answers with each method. I can't be sure when the Brin-Hask –"

"Tom," Dad interrupted. "Forget that for a minute. We've got something else to deal with."

Between them, Dad and Tom managed to get Charlie's rat out from under the colander and into the glass aquarium that had last housed Miss Ardman's preferred snacks – giant centipedes.

The rest of the rats had retreated back to their nest, abandoning the captive, and – this was the most worrying bit – replacing the wooden floorboards behind them.

In the library, the captured rat was at first frantic, searching for an escape. But when it realized there was none, it sat down in one corner and stared balefully at the watching humans. It twiddled the claws of its front paws, looking down at them now and then as though thinking, and then flicking them again.

"It's counting," Tom said. "Look, it's trying to figure something out."

The rat's eyes glowed steadily, and Amelia saw a flash of silver by its ear.

She pointed, "There, on the side of its head. It looks like –"

"It's a cyber-rat!" said Charlie. "Can I keep it?"

Mary swatted at him. "Get out of here!"

"I was only joking."

"Well, I'm not. In fact, both of you – here, take some money and go buy yourselves a hamburger or something down at the surf club. Leave us alone for a while to discuss things."

Amelia wanted to stay and listen, particularly if there was any chance her dad was going to jail, but Charlie had already snatched up the money and was out the door.

"Don't let my rat go," he called back. "I'm going to call him Hugo."

He was practically skipping over the grass, buzzing from the excitement of his rat capture. Amelia was solemn by comparison. Catching a rat wouldn't make up for anything when Mr. Snavely came back tomorrow.

She was walking slowly, thinking hard, when

she caught the flash of a dark shape out of the corner of her eye. She turned and saw the hem of a long, black coat flick around the corner of the hedge maze.

Without a second thought, she changed direction and sped towards the maze, not bothering to call out to Charlie and not bothering to answer when he yelled, "Hey! Where are you going?"

She didn't want to give whoever – *what*ever – was in the maze any tip-off that she was coming. She heard Charlie's footsteps behind her.

She sprinted into the maze, running the first long, straight pathway, then pausing in frustration at the corner where it branched in two. Charlie puffed up next to her, and Amelia held a warning finger to her lips.

"The guy in the black coat," she whispered. "He's here."

Obviously, the only chance they had to find him was to each take a different path, which meant they had to split up, but Amelia didn't care right now. With everything going to pieces up at the hotel, she was determined that at least one problem be solved. No way was another alien getting away with sneaking around behind her parents' backs.

Amelia went left, Charlie went right.

After three or four turns, Amelia lost her sense of direction. Every now and then, she and Charlie would cross paths, or she would hit a dead end and have to retrace her steps, but it was impossible to tell how much of the maze they had covered, or how close they were to finding the black coat.

She turned the next corner to find herself in the very center of the maze – a place she and Charlie had only stumbled on once before. There stood an old marble fountain in the middle of a reflection pond (now dry), and next to it, a stone bench on which to sit and think.

Sitting on the bench was a man in a long, black coat, his pockets bulging with eucalyptus leaves. As Amelia stared he looked over at her, casually took a leaf from his pocket and nibbled on it.

Charlie crashed in from the other side of the maze. "Who are you?" he asked bluntly.

"He's Tom's other arrival," said Amelia. "Aren't you?"

The man smiled, completely unconcerned. "There *has* been a containment breach, hasn't there?"

"Yeah, that's us," said Charlie. "A pair of breaches. So what are you?"

"Oh, I'm nobody from nowhere. Really. You should probably forget you ever saw me."

"I don't think so," said Amelia. "All the hotel guests have to sign the register. We have to remember everybody."

"But I'm not a hotel guest."

"But you came through the gateway!"

"Oh, yes."

"Then you have to register!" Amelia insisted. "Those are the rules! You'll get my dad in trouble if you don't sign in."

The man smiled. "It'll be far more trouble if I do. No, no, better we all forget we ever saw each other, I think."

Amelia was so angry, she shouted. "They're going to close us down! They're going to put my dad in jail, and you're making it worse!"

"Close you down? And what? Put in some of their Control stooges instead? Oh, no, that won't do. I don't think Lady Naomi would like it, either. No, I won't have it."

"What's it to do with you?" Charlie said rudely.

"It's all to do with me," the man said, gazing at Charlie with unblinking black eyes, his white face quite serious now.

"Yeah, right," Charlie snorted.

The man stood up abruptly. He was very tall, much taller than Amelia had guessed when he was sitting. His coat fell straight to his ankles, and was surely much too hot for today.

"You don't know who I am," he said simply. "But you have already formed an opinion of me?"

"Pretty much," said Charlie. "You're hiding in a maze with a coat stuffed full of leaves, and you reckon the stuff at the hotel is all to do with you."

The man arched an eyebrow and smiled without friendliness. "I hope you will not be so quick to judge the Brin-Hask when they arrive, Charlie. Thank you both for the mayonnaise. And don't look so worried, Amelia, this will all work out. You don't need to tell anyone about me, because I'm leaving now."

As lightly as a grasshopper he sprang into the

air, over their heads and the nearest hedge wall, and disappeared from sight.

Charlie gaped after him. Then, as though determined not to be impressed, he shook his head and called out, "Yeah, whatever. Bye, *Leaf Man.*"

CHAPTER FIVE

Going down to the beach for a hamburger didn't seem that relevant when you'd just seen an alien bounce twelve feet straight up in the air and vanish back into the maze you were still stuck in – an alien who'd just casually called you by name even though you'd never met before. For a long moment, Amelia and Charlie just stood there, afraid to move in case they were about to walk into an ambush.

In the end, Charlie said, "Oh, let's go. If he wanted to eat our brains with mayonnaise, he could have easily done it right here."

This disgusting piece of logic made sense to Amelia, and together they made their way out. By the time they emerged onto the lawn, Tom was limping back down the hill to his cottage.

Charlie gazed longingly back up to the hotel – wanting another peek at Hugo the rat, Amelia guessed – but sighed, and said, "Probably easier to get information out of Tom than our parents, don't you think?"

"Yeah."

It wasn't as though Tom liked them. He barely tolerated them being around, unless there was a job in town he needed doing, but he had one big attribute in his favor: he didn't go easy on them just because they were kids. He might keep secrets for his own reasons, but he never hid the truth to "protect" them, like their parents did.

So they went downhill to Tom's.

They caught up with him as he was closing his

front door.

"What now?" he grunted.

"We just met your mate, Leaf Man," said Charlie.

Tom stared. "Who?"

"The tall guy in the black coat," said Amelia. "He was lurking around the maze."

Tom groaned in exasperation and opened the door again. "Get inside. And don't *touch* anything, Charlie."

Amelia stepped as carefully as she could among the clutter and said, "Is everything OK up there?"

"No," Tom said bluntly. "A phone call came. Snavely is going to bring one of the senior managers from Control. Someone with the authority to make a binding decision."

"Oh." Amelia wished there were somewhere she could sit down and process that thought, but Tom didn't offer to clear a space on his sofa for them.

"Well?" he said, leaning against the door frame.

"We just want to know who Leaf Man is," said Charlie. "And what's up with those rats?"

"And what will happen to the hotel if we lose it," Amelia added. "And why Leaf Man won't sign the register."

"Right," Tom grunted. "Let's see. Well, half of it I can't tell you because I don't know myself, and the other half I won't tell you because it's none of your business. How's that?"

"Does my dad know about Leaf Man?"

Tom shrugged. "I don't know. He might."

"So would it be OK if I asked him?"

Tom stood upright and glowered at her. "Don't play games with me, missy. In case you haven't noticed, what you two know and who you blab it to is the whole reason we're in trouble here."

Amelia blanched, but Charlie retorted, "That's not true at all. You're just happy to blame us because it makes everyone forget it was *you* who started it! You were the one who went psycho and stole the eggs out of Miss Ardman's room! Plus, *we're* not the ones who let a bunch of cyborg rats in through the gateway!"

Tom turned purple, and was undoubtedly about to bellow at Charlie in unforgiveable language, except at that very second, the entire house shuddered on its foundations and the gateway beneath them belched out a cloud of icy air.

Tom growled. "Already?"

"The Brin-Hask!" said Charlie. "Can we stay? Please?" he begged, all manners and sweetness now. "We won't get in the way, we promise."

Amelia didn't think watching an army of alien warriors arrive from another galaxy would be the best way to relax after the day's adventures, but Charlie had already bunkered down on the arm of the sofa. She edged over to the wall and tried to look inconspicuous.

"Fine," Tom grumbled. "But listen up: the Brin-Hask have suffered a terrible defeat in battle. Not only are they exhausted, injured and far from home, they're also pretty hacked off about being beaten. Which is to say, *watch out*. They won't have any patience with you if they feel the slightest bit disrespected or insulted. Understand?"

Charlie nodded. "Don't annoy the angry soldiers. Got it."

Amelia just shivered.

And then they waited. And waited.

"How long –" Charlie started, but Tom hissed, "Shh!"

So they waited some more.

It was weird, Amelia thought. Were the Brin-Hask ghosts? Or made of vapor? If they were here, why couldn't they see them? Or even hear them? Maybe they were liquid, and were flowing silently up the stairs against gravity.

As Charlie started to fidget, something moved at the top of the stone steps. Amelia blinked and tried to focus harder. Yes – there it moved again. Something about the size of a sugar cube, only purple. And as it grew, or rather, as it moved, Amelia could see it was part of something larger – an arm?

Yes, an arm, and it was followed by a head, and the rest of a body, all densely furred like purple velvet. The alien, about as tall as a pigeon but shaped like a miniature bear, got to its feet and immediately turned to help up the next one.

This one was slightly shorter, with a silver shield strapped to its back. Its fur was the color of bubble gum.

"Wha–" said Charlie, but Tom poked him before he could go on.

Amelia put a hand over her mouth to hide her

smile. There were now half a dozen little bear-men at the top of the steps, and each one was fuzzier and sweeter than the last. Now one popped up that was a pale-pink tabby, and she gave a little moan of delight. Tom gave her a hard, beady look, and shook his head.

In all, fifty or sixty Brin-Hask "warriors" heaved themselves up the stone steps into Tom's house. After everything they'd been through, those stairs must have been like climbing Mount Everest. The last alien to arrive had extremely long fur, almost white, and the others fell back to make a path for him as he crossed the room to Tom.

Tom dropped awkwardly to one knee and bowed his head. "Hail, King Hibble. We are honored to have you stay with us."

King Hibble nodded graciously. "Greetings, Tom. Thank you for your welcome. We, however, have no honor – until we can avenge our disgrace, we are nothing in our own eyes."

He spoke nobly, with a kind of brooding melancholy, and a sword hung across his back. He also sounded like a cartoon mouse. Amelia wanted to cuddle him up. Charlie elbowed her roughly in the side, and she realized she must have let that thought show.

"Your grace," said Tom, wobbling slightly on that bended knee and sounding very weird as he

67

tried to be polite, "we have the, uh, grass of the sea you requested for the warriors' feast. Let me send these children ahead to begin the preparations."

"Fine," said Charlie promptly. "Come on, Amelia."

Amelia didn't think that sounded respectful at all, but followed him to the doorway. Tom hurried them outside and whispered, "Tell your dad he's got about three hours before the Brin-Hask arrive. And they'll want to pitch camp outside on the lawn."

"But –" Amelia knew they could ferry the entire army up to the hotel in a couple of cardboard boxes in less than ten minutes. Then she saw the look on Tom's face, and said, "Nothing. Sorry."

"Do they get holo-emitters?" said Charlie. "Do you have that many?"

Tom shook his head. "Not that many, and they wouldn't be effective at that scale. The holo-emitters only mask a person's shape, they can't change their size."

"So how do we, you know, keep our cover?" said Amelia.

Tom didn't answer, just grumbled to himself and shut the door, dismissing them.

"Pathetic," said Charlie, stamping his way through the dry leaves. "Worst warriors ever."

Amelia didn't mind. It was a relief to have just one thing today that was a *smaller* deal than expected.

CHAPTER SIX

The three parents were still in the library when Amelia and Charlie got back to the hotel, only now Mary had her shoes off and was lying with her feet up on the arm of the sofa by the fireplace. Mum was putting ice into a drink and Dad was drumming his fingers on the desk while he stared at the cyber-rat in its tank. Amelia noticed the rat was drumming its claws against the glass in time with him.

"Hugo!" said Charlie fondly. "Has anyone fed you yet?"

Dad gave him a look.

"Well, I'm starving," said Charlie. "Why wouldn't he be?"

"Why are you starving?" said Mary. "What did you do with the money I gave you?"

"We didn't go down to the bay," said Charlie.

"We were down at Tom's," said Amelia quickly, not sure why she was skipping over the Leaf Man part.

"Well, you'll have to wait about ..." Mum checked her watch, "another ten minutes. James has gone to get pizza because your dad's scared to go back in the kitchen to cook dinner."

"I'm not scared!" Dad protested, then added with dignity, "I'm terrified."

"Fair enough, too," said Mum, lifting her drink in salute.

"So what's going to happen to the Brin-Hask's feast?" said Amelia.

"It's all covered," said Dad. "We've ordered

thirty-eight family-sized pizzas. That should be enough for every soldier to have half a pizza, with plenty left over for us."

"I'll say!" Charlie snorted.

"What do you mean?"

"Didn't Tom tell you anything about the Brin-Hask?"

"Only how many were coming."

Charlie hooted, and Mum raised her eyebrows at Amelia. "Well?"

"They're very small, Mum."

"You mean, they're *micro*," said Charlie.

"Well, at least we haven't under ordered," said Mary.

It wasn't until James pulled up and started unloading the trunk that Amelia appreciated just how much food thirty-eight family-sized pizzas was. The whole lobby was filled with the smell of hot cheese and bread crusts. It was fantastic.

It was amazing how quickly hot food could cheer you up when you were seriously hungry. For the first time all day, Amelia began to feel a bit more hopeful about Mr. Snavely's return the next day. Leaf Man said it would be OK – and who knew? Maybe he was right.

Then James, chowing his way through a slab of anchovy pizza, broke off a chunk of crust and took the lid off the top of the cyber-rat's tank.

"Here you go, little buddy," James said, dropping it in.

"James, no! Don't –" shouted Dad, but the rat had already leapt onto James's wrist, raced up his arm and launched itself off his shoulder. Sailing across the room like a furry ballistic missile, it landed square on the rug next to Mary before bolting out to the kitchen.

"... take the lid off the tank," Dad finished faintly.

The pizza was cold by the time King Hibble and his warriors finally staggered through the daffodils and reached the main steps of the hotel, and the sun had set long ago. Amelia and Charlie were waiting for them. They had spread out an old picnic blanket on the grass and put four pizzas in the middle, with a bowl of water for the soldiers to refill their canteens.

The soldiers all but fell on the pizzas and after only a few minutes Amelia knew she'd have to go and get at least eight more. Small as they were, the Brin-Hask ate like piranhas. When at last they had rolled onto their backs, patting their stomachs, King Hibble clapped his paws and called, "Enrick! Enrick the bard – where are you? Your king wants a poem!"

Charlie groaned quietly. "Singing?" he whispered

to Amelia. "Poetry?" Then he mouthed silently, *lame*.

"Your grace," Enrick stood, a little stringed instrument in his paws, "what will you hear?"

"'The Ballad of Queen Gorrick and the Grawk,'" said King Hibble.

The soldiers all murmured their approval, but Charlie rolled his eyes.

Enrick coughed once, strummed his tiny instrument and began to sing in a high, beautiful voice a story that was so frightening, all the hair stood up on Amelia's arms. It began with a Grawk invading the Brin-Hask's land. Enrick didn't say what a Grawk was, but it sounded monstrous: a huge creature, as large as ten Brin-Hask warriors, with pure-black fur and eyes that glowed like molten metal. It was silent, cunning, and so quick that no one even saw its shadow before it fell on them. It avoided every trap, outsmarted every ambush and was stronger than every weapon.

Amelia was entranced until she saw King Hibble walking towards them.

"I'm sorry, sir," she said. "Is it rude to listen? We can go away."

But even as she was saying it, she was listening to Enrick describing how Queen Gorrick went out to take on the Grawk in single combat.

"No, cub," said the king. "But I have a question for you."

Amelia nodded.

"When you left us at the gateway, and ran ahead to prepare for our arrival – was not the grass of the sea prepared for my warriors?"

"Oh." Amelia gulped. "Yes. Lots of it."

"But we did not have it."

"No."

King Hibble looked at her silently, his little button eyes stern. Amelia tried again.

"No, sir. Your highness."

"What happened?"

"The rats," said Charlie bluntly.

"What is *rats*?"

"Oh, vicious things," said Charlie. "Well, normal rats are vicious, but these are even worse. They're some kind of alien cyber-rats, and they've taken over the hotel. Amelia's dad won't let us into the kitchen, where we left the seaweed."

King Hibble looked sharply at Amelia. "You've been forced out of your home by these creatures?"

Amelia nodded. "Yes, sir. And tomorrow the Control people are coming to throw us out. Or into jail. We don't know yet."

All the fur on King Hibble's body bristled. His eyes glinted, and he turned back to the picnic blanket of drowsy soldiers.

"Warriors of Brin-Hask!" he shouted.

Enrick the bard stopped singing, and instantly every warrior was on their feet and at attention.

"Tonight we were denied our traditional feast of the grass of the sea – denied it by a plague of filth that has fallen on this house!"

There was a general grumbling and jostling among the soldiers.

"A plague," the king went on, "that has driven these massive humans from their home, and will tomorrow result in their shame and expulsion. Do you know what this means?"

The warriors shouted in excitement, and Amelia saw swords and clubs waved in the air, shields raised and clanged together.

"Yes!" King Hibble cried. "We have a foe worthy of battle! We have a chance to burn away our disgrace, and if any of us live to tell the tale, we will return to our homes with glory! For we have a *fight to the death!*"

King Hibble blew a hunting horn, and the warriors leapt into rough lines.

"Charge!" he screamed, and the mass of tiny, colorful warriors swarmed across the lawn and up the steps. They swept past Amelia and Charlie in a wave of fury and disappeared through the front doors of the hotel.

Amelia blinked. The Brin-Hask could move with incredible speed when they had a battle to win. She and Charlie scrambled to their feet and ran after them.

CHAPTER SEVEN

Amelia and Charlie raced along the veranda after the charging Brin-Hask army, almost knocking over the card table the parents were sitting at.

"Hey!" Dad yelled. "What are you doing?"

"Charlie!" Mary was shocked. "Are you chasing those aliens?"

"Not chasing, following," Charlie corrected her over his shoulder.

"They're attacking the rats," Amelia yelled back, already in the lobby where the Brin-Hask were now paused – scouts jogging off towards the library in one direction, the ballroom in another.

"It's straight ahead!" Amelia called. "Follow the seaweed smell!"

"I'll get the door for them," said Charlie, but instead of racing after the army he stopped dead and stared up at the gallery. Amelia followed his gaze and her mouth fell open. After a day where she had seen the kitchen floor vomit up ranks of cyber-rats, and met the universe's cutest-slash-most-bloodthirsty creatures, with a strange bouncing alien in a maze in between, there ought to have been nothing much that could surprise Amelia.

But there she was: Lady Naomi herself.

She was standing in the gallery and gazing down at them. Amelia just stared. She was really there. A young woman, straight backed and graceful even in the way she held herself, like a dancer on stage. Or a ninja. She had slanting gray eyes, long black hair and an elegance that reminded Amelia of the foreign dignitaries Mum had sometimes worked with as a diplomat.

For once, Amelia couldn't blame James for falling in love at first sight. Not that James would ever have a hope with a woman like this.

As Lady Naomi stepped closer to the railing, light fell on a long, twisted scar that ran from the shoulder of her right arm, down to the wrist. It was raised and jagged, as though the healing had been difficult. Yet somehow, she made even that terrible injury look glamorous.

"Did I really just see the warriors of Brin-Hask streaking past?" she asked. Even her voice was lovely.

Amelia nodded, and then cleared her throat. "Yes!"

"What are they doing? You didn't offend them, did you?"

"Not us!" said Charlie. "They're after the rats!"

Lady Naomi let out a stifled squawk of excitement and rushed down the stairs. Despite her haste, she moved as silently and fluidly as a cat. When she reached the lobby, grinning brilliantly, she stood between Charlie and Amelia – a little taller than Charlie, an inch or so shorter than Amelia – and seized their hands in hers.

Before Amelia could process the fact that not only was Lady Naomi real, but actually touching her, she was being dragged off to the kitchen.

"Come on," Lady Naomi cried. "We'll never see anything like this again, I promise!"

They burst into the kitchen through the empty doorway that once housed the kitchen door, now shattered to pieces by Brin-Hask axes. The warriors were already arranged around the loose floorboards by the oven. Nothing had happened yet, but there was the same intense excitement in the air as if a bomb were about to explode.

King Hibble glanced up at them. "My lady, you look well. Keep the cubs out of the way, will you?"

"Yes, your grace." She curtsied, then said, "All right, we need to get up off the ground."

They climbed onto the far counter, Charlie standing in the sink like Mr. Snavely had, Amelia sitting on the draining board with her feet tucked under her. Lady Naomi sat on the wooden bread box, and after looking around, armed herself with a long knife sharpener. They had a perfect view of the whole kitchen.

At a signal from King Hibble, the front line of his warriors approached the floorboards and began levering them up with their swords. Before they had lifted as much as the corner, though, the whole section of floor exploded up from below – not just the couple of boards that had been moved when Dad and Mr. Snavely investigated,

but almost a three-foot square blasted out. The entire Brin-Hask army was caught out – the back lines thrown violently against the walls, the rest tumbling down into the gaping cavity that had opened below them.

Taken by surprise, and all but knocked out by the force of the explosion, falling helplessly into a pit of enraged, glowing-eyed cyber-rats, King Hibble and his army simply disappeared.

Charlie sucked in a breath. "It's going to be a massacre!"

The remaining Brin-Hask warriors staggered to their feet, obviously partly concussed. They gathered up their weapons and, without a word, charged back towards the hole in the floor, diving into the abyss to join their comrades.

"It's going to be carnage," Amelia whispered, horrified.

Lady Naomi gave a wicked grin. "Yeah."

CHAPTER EIGHT

The kitchen was filled with screams of outrage. It was impossible to know what was going on, as the battle was all below the floor, but Amelia quickly learned to tell the difference between the high-pitched squeals of the rats and the joyous battle cries of the Brin-Hask. All they saw were the long, scaly rat tails as they flicked past the blast hole, and the occasional flash of a sword or shield.

Then a massive thump shook the hotel, and all the floorboards in the kitchen pulverized –

instantly dissolving into dust and falling back into the cavity.

"What was that?" Charlie yelped. "Did the Brin-Hask do that?"

Lady Naomi laughed in amazement. "I don't know. The Brin-Hask don't use bombs or machinery of any kind, although they know how to manage them when they find them."

"The rats had rigged the whole floor to explode?" said Amelia.

"It looks like it," said Lady Naomi. "Probably supposed to be a last resort for mass escape if they ever needed to flee the hotel. I doubt it offers them much advantage in a fight like this."

"Then why did they set it off now?" said Charlie.

"They probably didn't. I imagine the Brin-Hask decided to see what would happen if they triggered it."

"What?" Charlie gaped. "The Brin-Hask set

off a bomb without knowing what it would do? Are they crazy?"

"A little bit," Lady Naomi smiled. "They can't stand suspense but they love chaos – setting off the bomb put the fight more on their terms."

"You mean ..." Amelia paused as she took in the new scene of battle. From under the thick layer of wood dust that had fallen into the cavity, hundreds of small furry bodies leapt up once more, shook themselves off, and threw themselves back into combat. Now that she could see the entire arena of the war, she realized it was even worse than it had sounded. The rats were far larger than the Brin-Hask – more heavily built, and there were many, many times more of them. The sixty-odd little aliens were swamped.

Here and there, Amelia saw two of the Brin-Hask stand back-to-back, holding off a circle of ten or more attacking rats. One warrior was snatched up in a rat's mouth, and kept slashing at it with his sword even as it shook him like a doll. The rats kept coming – up out of the ground, their eyes all shining red, and every now and then she caught a flash of silver from their electronic implants. For all Amelia knew, they could communicate with each other instantly – how could the Brin-Hask compete with that?

And yet somehow, she noticed, the number of dead rats was growing. Where there had first been nothing but seething movement, now there were little islands of slumped bodies.

"You mean," Amelia said, wondering, "the Brin-Hask could actually win this?"

"Without a doubt," said Lady Naomi.

Charlie cheered as a great chunk of rat fur and whiskers flew into the air off a Brin-Hask sword, and Amelia felt a tremor of excitement.

Another explosion shook the kitchen, this one

spraying out a stinging cloud of gravel. Amelia coughed and wiped dust out of her eyes with her T-shirt.

"How many bombs do they have?" Charlie spluttered, half fuming, half admiring.

Quite a few, it turned out. None as devastating as the first one that had disintegrated the floor, but all of them nasty.

"How can the Brin-Hask match this?" Amelia asked Lady Naomi, but Lady Naomi just nodded and said, "Watch."

As she watched, Amelia began to notice a pattern. A bomb went off every time an attack by the rats failed. They would rally in their perfect lines, charge shoulder to shoulder against the Brin-Hask, and try to overpower them with numbers, but the sheer fury of the Brin-Hask swords drove them back every time. Each time the rats retreated, they would make up for the loss by triggering another bomb.

And the blasts were getting closer together. What had at first sounded like the thundering superiority of the rat forces was actually proof that the Brin-Hask were gaining ground.

"They're winning!" Amelia cheered. "The Brin-Hask are going to win!"

Another bomb blast splintered all the cupboard doors, and the counter they were all sitting on rocked alarmingly. This was followed almost immediately by another cloud of gravel, and the rats seemed on the verge of panic. They weren't holding their formations anymore, and were even scrambling over one another in their desperation to get away from the Brin-Hask.

"It's over," said Lady Naomi. "King Hibble won't fight them once their defense has collapsed. Look – can you see him there with his broadsword? He's going to call for their surrender and start taking prisoners."

But as King Hibble raised his voice to shout out his willingness to show mercy, there was a harsh fizzing noise and all the lights in the kitchen flickered, then went out.

"What's this?" roared King Hibble.

The fizzing noise grew louder and in the dark, Amelia saw all the glowing red rats' eyes flicker and die. Without the glowing eyes, she could see nothing, not even the moon outside gave any light, but the air around her began to thicken with the foul, wet smell of burnt fur, and here and there came a slow sizzling pop, as though something big had flown into a bug zapper.

When the lights came back on, King Hibble stood astounded, before his face fell in disgust. Every rat lay dead on the ground, electrocuted and slightly smoking.

"The rats exploded themselves?" said Charlie.

"Maybe," said Lady Naomi. "Or someone else did."

"Who?" said Amelia. "Not King Hibble?"

Lady Naomi shook her head. "Never. None of the Brin-Hask would act so dishonorably."

"Then who?"

"A good question. Perhaps if we knew who put the cybertronics into ordinary Earth rats in the first place?"

"They weren't alien rats?" Amelia asked.

"No, poor things. They were just the hosts for someone else's technology. Right now, though, I don't know who that someone else would be, or what they were trying to achieve. The only thing we can tell from this is that they would rather destroy their entire operation than risk having us capture even a single rat intact."

"But I did!" Charlie said. "I caught Hugo and we put him in a tank!"

Lady Naomi beamed at him. "You did? Oh, well done! If we can –"

"James, let it go," Charlie interrupted her, his excitement gone.

Lady Naomi looked stricken, something deeper than disappointment, almost a grief in her eyes. Then she forced herself to smile, and said, "Ah, well. I see. Never mind." She stretched and stood up on the counter, then lightly leapt down to one of the exposed beams in the destroyed floor, landing as neatly as an acrobat. "Is there any pizza left?"

She picked her way across the battlefield, hopping from beam to beam and balancing with no apparent effort. At the doorway to the hall she turned back and bowed to the Brin-Hask, who waved her good-bye from the now rather gruesome mess that was the cavity under the floor.

Charlie leaned over the edge of his sink and

surveyed the damage. Clumps of fur, spatters of blood and the corpses of slaughtered rats lay all over the kitchen. The combined stench of blood, guts, singed hair and burnt barbecue was unbearable. It was hard to imagine anyone ever being able to cook in there again. In the midst of it all, the Brin-Hask laughed and cheered and pestered Enrick the bard for another story.

"That," said Charlie, "was the most amazing thing I've ever seen."

"Yes," said Amelia, still gazing after Lady Naomi, "she really is."

Dad could only laugh – not a particularly happy laugh, more the helpless, hysterical kind – when he saw what had happened to his kitchen. When he remembered that Mr. Snavely would be back the next morning with a Control superior, he peeled off into wild giggles.

"Well, we can't hide it," said Mum. "We can't fix it or change it, so there's no use worrying about it."

"So what do we do?" asked Mary.

"Right now, we turn our backs on it."

James hadn't said a word. He'd stood in mute shock as the Brin-Hask warriors marched past him on their way back to their picnic blanket. He'd just turned pale when he saw the kitchen.

Amelia felt sorry for him. She could see it was almost physically hurting him to accept that he'd been wrong, and the aliens were real. Changing his whole view of the world to include the existence of an interstellar gateway at the bottom of his garden was not easy.

She wondered if changing his mind would change his attitude, too. It'd be nice if he could stop being a mega-jerk and go back to being the more or less decent big brother she remembered.

He saw her looking at him and said, "What do you want?" Without waiting for a reply, he turned and stomped upstairs to his room. She heard a door slam and, a few seconds later, the din of music being played way too loud.

Amelia shook her head and walked out to the veranda. Lady Naomi had fetched the Brin-Hask their seaweed at last, and they were sitting around a campfire they had built on a paving stone, and roasting it on the end of sticks – the same way Amelia would roast marshmallows. Enrick the bard was singing again, and when he got to the chorus, all the warriors joined in, trilling like canaries in beautiful harmonies:

Kill, kill, kill them all dead!
Give me an ax and I'll hack off his head!
So, kill, kill, kill!

Charlie was humming along with them.

It was all as cheerful, grisly, fun, weird, amazing, and kind of gross and unnerving as Amelia had come to expect of the Gateway Hotel. She looked around, feeling very fond of the place, and sad that they'd probably all be fired (or in jail) by this time tomorrow.

At the corner of the hotel Amelia saw a shadow flit past, a black coat billowing behind and the flash of a white face as Leaf Man glanced back the way he'd come. He looked satisfied.

CHAPTER NINE

Amelia slept late the next day. The Brin-Hask celebrations had gone on far into the night, and Mum and Dad – knowing it could be their last night at the hotel – had let Amelia stay up to enjoy it. Mary hadn't tried to argue with Charlie, she just agreed straightaway that yes, he could stay the night too. None of them had slept much, what with the intensity of the battle behind them, the dread of the day ahead of them, and in between – those eerily sweet yet murderous songs of the Brin-Hask, and the pretty revolting stench of burning seaweed.

The sun was high in the sky before Amelia stirred. Charlie was still fast asleep on the guest bed and seemed determined to stay that way, no matter how hard Amelia poked him.

"Leave me alone!" he groaned into his pillow.

"Don't you want to check out the kitchen?" Amelia goaded him. "Look for the control center or whatever linked all the cyber-rats? Check for unexploded bombs?"

Charlie sat up with a jerk, his face alight with possibility, but then a thought flickered in his eyes, and he said dully, "No, you do it. I'll come down later."

Amelia frowned at him. "You *don't* want to pick through rat carcasses and hunt for weapons?"

"No." He didn't meet her eye.

"Charlie?"

"Later!" He thudded back onto his pillow,

rolled over and started fake snoring until Amelia left him to it.

Downstairs the kitchen looked worse than she'd remembered. At night, under electric light and with the smoke still lifting into the air, it had been impressive and dramatic. In the morning sunlight, though, it was just a filthy mess. Dad's shoulders slumped as he gazed at it, and Mum patted his back gently.

"When does Mr. Snavely get here?" said Amelia.

"About twenty minutes," said Dad.

"Do you know who he's bringing with him?" Mum asked.

Dad shook his head. "One of the big three. If it's Arxish, we're done for. He's wanted the gateway run by Control for years, and any excuse will do. If it's Stern, we've got a chance – he's sympathetic to leaving gateways to the locals, as long as they're up to it." He made a miserable face at that. "But if it's the new one, Rosby – I don't know. No one knows much about her yet."

"Will we really go to jail, Dad?"

"Oh, no!" He managed a smile at that. "I'm sure not. Mr. Snavely is always threatening stuff like that. He wishes he had that sort of power but no, it's not up to him to send anyone to jail."

"But," Amelia pressed on, "we're fired, aren't we?"

He sighed. "I hope not, but ... it doesn't look good. Sorry, kiddo. Still –" he hesitated, trying to look on the bright side. "Moving back home to the city wouldn't be the *worst* thing in the world, would it?"

"I should be so lucky." James stumped along the hallway, his hair all bed-tangled, and pale, skinny legs sticking out of his striped boxer shorts.

Mum looked at him in amusement. "Good morning, sunshine. Mr. Snavely will be here any minute now. Do you want to put some pants on before he comes?"

Amelia looked down at her own grubby pajamas and decided real clothes would be better for her, too. She padded back to the lobby, her bare feet silent on the marble stairs up to her room – and realized with a start how much it really did feel like *her* room. Already, going back to the city would be like going back to someone else's life.

She was halfway along the gallery when she heard a floorboard squeak – but not under *her* foot.

She skipped the last couple of feet to the head of the hallway and saw Charlie creeping out of James's room, easing the door closed behind him.

"Charlie!"

He spasmed in shock. "Amelia! Don't do that! Kids can have heart attacks too, you know."

"What were you doing in my brother's room?"

Charlie grinned and held up the holo-emitter. "Got it!"

"You can't do that!"

"I just did."

"But you shouldn't have."

"But I did."

It could have developed into quite an argument, but Charlie seized on the sound of a car in the driveway and said, "They're here!"

Amelia fled to her room, slamming the door on Charlie and scrambling to get changed before she missed anything downstairs. She needn't have worried. It turned out to be Mary, coming back from Forgotten Bay with coffee for the adults and croissants and bagels all around. Charlie stayed close to his mum, pretending to be ravenous so that Amelia couldn't get close enough to continue the conversation.

But soon another car crunched up the driveway

and into the turning circle, and they heard the heavy clunk of Mr. Snavely's car doors being opened and closed.

Dad peered out the library window and groaned.

"Who is it?" said Mum.

"Rosby."

"Oh. What does she look like?"

"Not what I expected, to be honest."

Amelia looked. There was Mr. Snavely, as thin and sneering as the day before, and on the other side of the car, an ancient-looking woman, her gray hair curled into a bun, leaning on a cane. She tottered slowly around the car's long hood, but looked up brightly enough at the hotel.

"Showtime," whispered Dad.

He went to the lobby and opened the door, his usual smile faltering. "Good morning, Mr. Snavely. Good morning, Ms. Rosby."

Ms. Rosby made her way inside and nodded to all of them.

Mr. Snavely handed Dad a fat white envelope with a red seal. "My report on yesterday's inspection. Just a copy for your records, you understand," he said greasily. "The original has already been lodged with Control headquarters."

Dad gulped.

"Adrian says you've got a hive of robotically enhanced animals under the hotel?" said Ms. Rosby.

"Not anymore," said Dad.

"Don't suppose you managed to trap one, did you? Be jolly useful to have a specimen to send back to the lab."

"I did!" Charlie beamed. When Ms. Rosby turned to him, though, he was forced to add, "But it got away ..."

"Ah, I see. Pity."

Dad coughed. "The ... ah ... situation has ... *evolved* somewhat since yesterday."

"Oh?" Ms. Rosby cocked her head to one side, her eyes bright.

"Yes. You know the Brin-Hask arrived last night?"

"I thought I smelled seaweed!" Ms. Rosby looked delighted. "Marvelous. I'll have to pay my respects before we go, Snavely."

"Yes, well," Dad went on. "They heard about the rats."

"How?" said Mr. Snavely. He had his clipboard out and was taking notes already.

"The ..." Dad sighed. "The kids told them."

Mr. Snavely flashed a triumphant look at Ms. Rosby, but Ms. Rosby merely waited for Dad to go on.

Dad, however, was lost for words.

"Perhaps it's simplest if we just show you," Mum suggested.

She led them down the hallway and threw open the door to the kitchen. Mr. Snavely's mouth dropped open. The dust and smoke in the air had died away completely overnight, but the smell of burnt rats that replaced it was not an improvement. Mr. Snavely's eyes bulged, he gagged slightly, and put a white-gloved hand to his mouth in horror as he backed away from the room.

Ms. Rosby thumped the floor with her cane and cried, "Oh, bravo!"

"I beg your pardon?" said Dad.

"Really, brilliantly well done," Ms. Rosby said warmly. "Look, Snavely, get down there and fetch me one of those poor things, will you?"

"One of – what?" Mr. Snavely blinked at her. "Poor what?"

"A rat, Snavely. Get me a rat. Poor little wretches, I'm sure I've seen this sort of thing before. Go on, Snavely – what are you waiting for? You've got gloves on, haven't you?"

Almost whimpering in disgust, Mr. Snavely lowered himself into the ruined floor and picked up the matted, dusty body of a rat. It was slashed open along its belly.

Ms. Rosby took a thin metal gadget out of her jacket pocket and prodded the rat as it lay in Mr. Snavely's hand. The red eyes sparked with light, and the body twitched as machinery inside responded, but it was only the slightest of movements. When Ms. Rosby pressed a button on her gadget and prodded the rat a second time, there was a grinding noise and the red eyes died again.

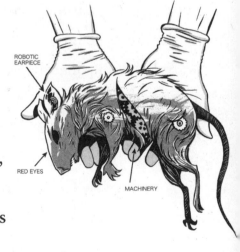

ROBOTIC
EARPIECE

RED EYES

MACHINERY

"Humph." She put the gadget back in her pocket, disappointed. "I suppose they destroyed the hive center?"

Dad looked blank.

"Yes," said Amelia. "At least, I think so. They kept setting off little bombs, but the last one electrocuted them all."

Ms. Rosby sighed. "Yes, they self-destruct every time. Ah well, can't be helped. The fact is, you got rid of them all, and that's as much as any of us in Control have been able to do so far."

"What?" Dad was trying to catch up. "Are you saying –"

"You handled the problem," said Ms. Rosby. "That's what you are here to do, isn't it? Handle problems? Well, then, what do you want me to say? Get on with it!"

"You mean ..." Dad was faint. "We can stay?"

"No!" said Mr. Snavely.

Ms. Rosby regarded him coolly. "Are you contradicting me?"

"But, but –" Mr. Snavely spluttered. "The children! The children are the problem! The rats were only discovered yesterday! It was the children Miss Ardman complained about."

"Yes, I read the reports, Snavely. I know the story as well as you do. As I understand it, the core issue was the caretaker falling under the spell of those eggs."

Mr. Snavely nodded.

"The man's first lapse in judgment in the thirty years he's been here," Ms. Rosby went on. "Am I right?"

Mr. Snavely nodded again.

"And something that could easily happen to any of us. In fact, Miss Ardman should consider herself lucky if Tom doesn't lodge a counter-complaint that she failed to protect him by not properly securing the eggs."

Mr. Snavely opened his mouth. He thought better of it, and closed it again.

"Furthermore," Ms. Rosby said crisply, "the issue with the *children*, as you call them, seems to be rather that they *weren't* informed about the gateway. Now that they know what's going on here, I see they are managing themselves and the situation as well as their parents. Perhaps even better." She smiled at Amelia and Charlie.

Mr. Snavely had had enough. "I must object! How can we trust Gateway Control's mission, its security, its *dignity*, I say, to those who are not yet ..." He faltered.

"Not yet what?" Ms. Rosby snapped.

Mr. Snavely was silent, his face pale and fearful. He looked as though he'd just realized a terrible mistake, but Amelia couldn't tell what it was.

Ms. Rosby turned to her, and smiled again.

"Tell me, my dear, how old would you guess I am?"

Amelia shook her head. There was no way to answer an age question politely. Whatever she said, it was bound to come out badly. But Charlie wasn't so restrained.

"Eighty-nine!" he said.

Ms. Rosby grinned. Mr. Snavely writhed.

"Not even close! Guess again."

"A hundred and four!" Charlie grinned back.

Ms. Rosby leaned over her cane, her wrinkles deepening as she smiled more broadly than ever and said, "Nope. I'm six years old. In Earth years, that is." She straightened up and gave Mr. Snavely a hard look. "And I'm quite capable of protecting Control's mission, secrecy *and* dignity, thank you."

She shook hands with Dad, who was so stunned he just stared at her, and Mum, who smiled calmly. Ms. Rosby said to Amelia and Charlie, "Lovely to meet you all. Scott, I'll send a crew in to clean up this mess. You should have a new kitchen installed within the week on my recommendation."

Dad stammered a bit, but nothing much came out.

"Come, Snavely," said Ms. Rosby. "And bring the rat. I want to thank the Brin-Hask for their superb work last night."

She tottered back out to the lobby, Mr. Snavely following her wretchedly, while Amelia and the others stood in silent amazement.

They were staying!

CHAPTER TEN

As soon as Mr. Snavely's car had disappeared from view, Mum and Dad broke into loud cheers. Dad swept Mum up in his arms and they danced around the lobby, laughing goofily. Mary sat down hard on the arm of a chair, limp with relief, while Charlie whooped and high-fived Amelia so many times, her palms were red.

James had stayed in his room for the whole event, and if he heard them at all, he was ignoring them.

Mum went to the cellar and came back with a

bottle of champagne. Then, looking at the kids, realized the box of extra-fancy chocolates she kept in her bottom drawer would be a better way for them to celebrate. Amelia was on her fourth caramel when Dad blurted out, "Tom! We haven't told Tom yet!"

Mum looked guilty, then said, "Quick, kids – go and get him for us, would you? He's part of this too."

Outside, Amelia looked around for the Brin-Hask. Their campsite seemed deserted.

"Have they gone already? I thought their wormhole didn't arrive until tonight."

"Don't you remember how long it took them to get up here?" said Charlie. "And it's probably like the airport – maybe Tom likes them there two hours early or something."

That made the trip down to Tom's a bit slower than usual. Normally they would have raced each other down the steep slopes, hardly looking where they were going, but now that they knew there was an army of tiny aliens plowing their way through the long grass, they moved much more cautiously.

"We should have mowed a pathway for them," said Charlie. "We kind of owe them that much."

They caught up to the warriors in the clearing outside Tom's cottage. Poor Enrick was being pestered by a dozen different suggestions for the new song he was trying to compose, "The Ballad of King Hibble and the Earth Rats." King Hibble himself was at the head of the procession, laughing with his companions. When they heard the kids coming through the leaf litter, the whole army turned.

This time, Amelia knew exactly what to do, and it didn't feel awkward at all. She dropped to one knee, bowed her head and said, "Your highness, you saved both our families. Thank you!"

The king laughed again. "Yes, Metti Rosby came to tell us as she left. We are pleased for you, cubs."

"But now you're going, and we haven't done anything for you," said Amelia.

"I've got a chocolate in my pocket," said Charlie. "You can have that."

"We have our honor back," said the king. "We can go home without shame. That is enough for us. And," he added, "Metti Rosby promised to send a crate-load of the Guild's best salted scorpions as thanks from Control."

A cheer went up from the warriors.

"You'd rather have salted scorpions than chocolate?" said Charlie.

The door of Tom's cottage opened with a creak.

"I thought I heard voices out here." Then Tom remembered who he was talking to. "Your grace."

"Did you hear we get to stay, too?" said Amelia.

"And Ms. Rosby said Amelia and I should get to know everything!" Charlie added.

Amelia didn't think that was quite what Ms. Rosby had said, but she let it go for now. Tom grunted.

"Did she come to see you too?"

He nodded. "Said she wanted to send someone to do up this place." He looked sullen. "Said it's not good enough for the most active gateway on this side of the galaxy to look like it's run out of a slum. A slum! Can you believe some people?"

Amelia thought of the plates of forgotten sandwiches. And the apple cores. And the open packages of cookies that lay among the piles of charts and clockwork. It said something, she thought, that even a nest of cyber-rats had preferred to live in a nearly empty hotel than come anywhere near Tom's squalor. She had no idea what the rats had been eating, but apparently it was better than any of Tom's leftovers.

Tom stood back from the door to let the Brin-Hask through, and just rolled his eyes as Amelia and Charlie followed them.

"So what will Control do to this place?" said Amelia.

"Nothing!" he growled. "I convinced her it was far safer to leave it as it is. If she does it up too flashy, well, that'd only raise suspicion if anyone from Forgotten Bay came looking, wouldn't it? Some old shack in the woods, and all clean and fancy inside?"

"Oh," said Charlie. "So all this mess is just a clever disguise, is it?"

Tom scowled at him.

The gateway grumbled.

"What time will our wormhole align?" said King Hibble.

"I'm not sure, your grace," said Tom, immediately polite. "The wormholes keep speeding up, but unpredictably. And as you know, the Brin-Hask connection is always unstable."

"Why?" said Charlie.

Tom glared, but the king answered him. "We come from one of the farthest reaches of the universe where gravity works slightly differently. It's stronger in our world, for one thing."

Charlie nodded. "Is that why you're all so short?"

Charlie! Amelia thought anxiously. *Why would you say that?*

But the king just nodded. "And, to be modest, why we are so strong. Your planet's gravity is like a shadow of what we are used to at home."

To make his point, he put a hand under the corner of Tom's sofa and lifted. Without any apparent effort he held one end of the sofa above his head. The other end was still on the ground but Amelia was in no doubt, he could have easily lifted all of the sofa's weight – it was only the size that was too much for his paws.

The gateway grumbled again, and this time Amelia heard the cawing of distant birds.

"It's here!" said Tom. "You have to go now."

Amelia wondered how sixty warriors could get down that long stone staircase quickly enough, but gravity was the answer there, too. King Hibble simply called out, "In ranks!" and the warriors fell into rough formation and jogged into the next room.

"Farewell!" the king cried and they ran, leaping, into the hole in the floor.

Charlie would have run forward after him to get a good look, but Tom caught the back of his shirt and said, "They practically bounce down. Imagine it for yourself, because you're going nowhere near those stairs."

Charlie frowned, but didn't argue for once. The gateway's grumble increased until the noise hurt their ears, and the door at the bottom of the stairs was sucked shut with a bang. The cottage was silent.

"Right, then," said Tom. "Off you go."

"Oh, that's nice," said Charlie. "And we only came to invite you to celebrate with us up at the house."

Tom snorted. "You can celebrate, I have work to do." He poked around the clutter on his desk and began fiddling with an old music box, undoing the screws.

"Will the Brin-Hask come back?" Amelia asked.

"Who can tell?" he shrugged. "But I wouldn't hold your breath. The Brin-Hask wormhole is not only unstable, it also moves very slowly."

"That doesn't make sense," said Charlie.

"It doesn't need to make sense to you!" Tom snapped. "I'm telling you how it is. The Brin-Hask connection with Earth only lines up every three or four years, so, no –" he looked at Amelia, "I wouldn't count on seeing the warriors again for a while."

"Three or four years," she said, thoughtfully. "I sort of thought aliens could travel whenever they liked."

"Don't you kids pay attention to anything that goes on here? The gateway operates on wormholes. No wormhole, no travel. The whole point of the hotel is that people have to *wait* for the right wormhole. The Brin-Hask and Miss Ardman stayed overnight, but some guests have to wait for weeks or months."

"But not Leaf Man," said Amelia.

"What?" Tom gaped.

"Leaf Man doesn't seem to wait. He doesn't stay at the hotel, and he told us he was leaving yesterday afternoon, but then I saw him again last night. Either he was lying about going or ... well, maybe he can control the wormholes."

Tom's face contorted alarmingly. "You – nosy – little –" he began.

Amelia thought it was a good time to go, before he finished that sentence. There was a violent bang as a blast of wind from the gateway blew open the door downstairs.

"What was that?" Charlie yelped.

Tom looked satisfied. "A blowback."

"A what?"

"A good lesson to you two not to get over-excited about the gateway – not to think you can just ask a couple of questions and know what's going on here."

"So what is going on?" said Amelia.

Tom looked stern. "A blowback is a reminder of how dangerous the gateway is. Not interesting, not amazing, and not *cool*." He sneered on the last word as only a grown-up who thought kids were idiots could. "It's none of those things. It's raw *danger*."

Charlie was thrilled. "But that *is* cool!"

"Listen to me!" Tom bellowed. "You don't know what a blowback is. You can't know!"

"So tell us," said Amelia.

"I am telling you! *No one* can know. A blowback can be literally anything in the universe – anything that has wandered too close to a shifting wormhole and gotten sucked into the current it creates after itself. Downstairs, the door was ripped open by wind. Now," he said more calmly, "it could be that it was *only* wind – a gust of air trapped in the wrong place and escaping here. Noisy, but more or less harmless."

Charlie sniggered.

Tom, ignoring him, went on. "But it could have carried anything at all with it. Sometimes, I have been down the stairwell and it's been full of fish. Or alien leaves. Or enormous shoes. Once there was half a tree – only half, split down the middle from leaves to roots, as though the wormhole had sliced it through like a laser. And that could have easily have been a person standing there. So do you see? There could be *any*thing at the bottom of the stairs."

Amelia said meekly, "So how do you find out?"

Tom looked bleak. "How do you think? I go and look."

Amelia stared at him: an eye patch, a hand missing a finger, the limp that Charlie believed was a wooden leg. How much of that had been the gateway?

He sighed deeply and fetched a climbing

harness from behind the sofa. It was attached to a rope that was bolted to the floor with a heavy iron ring. He strapped himself into the harness, tugged on the rope and then said, "You both stay in this room, understand? Not a single toe beyond the doorway. And if I am longer than a minute, or if I yell out, or if you hear anything that isn't me, you *go*. Don't hesitate. You run, close the door behind you and go straight to your parents. Right?"

"Promise," said Amelia.

Tom grumbled to himself and limped towards the stairwell. Halfway there, he paused. The gateway had been still since that last bang, so he continued over to the top of the stairs. The rope had been tied so he had just enough length to make it across the room and down the stairs. Amelia watched it slither across the floor after him, uncoiling, straightening and then tightening as he reached the bottom. They heard the door close – carefully, not slammed shut by the wind, so it must have been Tom – and then the thud of his boots returning up the stairs.

When he emerged from the stairwell, he was in his undershirt, carrying his shirt rolled up in a bundle.

"What's that?" said Charlie.

Tom carried the bundle over to the kitchen table, shoving aside some plates. "Shut the door, Charlie. Let's not let anything in or out of here until we know what we've got."

Charlie pushed the door closed and Amelia crossed her arms, uncertain. It didn't smell like dead fish. It was smaller than a tree. That still left a lot of things in the universe it could be.

Tom unwrapped the corner of his shirt, and out popped a square, black head, softly furred with two enormous yellow eyes.

"What's that?" said Charlie.

The eyes blinked and then a wide, toothy mouth opened in a yawn, revealing a long, purple tongue.

"It's a puppy!" said Amelia, and ignoring Tom's gruff, "Hey!" she stepped forward and lifted the little animal into her arms. She gazed at it, taking in the stout body, the fat paws and the soft black fur. The animal gazed back, cocking its ears intelligently.

"That's not a puppy," said Charlie. "It's an alien."

The creature turned its head and looked balefully at him.

"It's a creepy alien," he corrected himself.

"Don't be silly," said Amelia. "He's lovely." She snuggled her face against his fur.

"Don't do that!" snapped Tom. "You don't know where it's been!"

"Don't know where he's *from*," Amelia said. "So what do we do with him?"

"I'll have to contact Control," said Tom. "Search the databases, match the description and find its origin. There's all probability that it's from the Brin-Hask planet, but we'll have to verify that officially. Unless the thing can talk for itself ..."

He regarded it for a moment, but it only wagged its tail and tucked its head trustingly under Amelia's chin.

"What will Control do with him?" she asked.

Tom *ummed* and *ahhed* a bit. "They'll most likely order us to negate the security breach."

Amelia looked at him steadily. "Meaning?"

"Meaning," Tom admitted, "that they'll send someone to put it down."

"Oh, no, that won't happen," Amelia said. "I'll keep him. Dad said I could get a dog anyway."

"Hmm," said Charlie. "It's not exactly a dog, though, is it?"

Of course it wasn't a dog. His glowing yellow eyes had vertical slits for pupils, like a cat's, and he smelled more like the beach than an actual dog. And rather than yapping his head off and trying to bite and chew everything in reach, he was cuddling quietly into her arms. But those didn't seem like reasons to let Control kill him. If anything, didn't they make him more precious? More deserving of her protection?

"I'm keeping him," she said. "That's all."

The little creature opened its mouth into a wide, happy smile and barked, just once:

"*Grawk!*"

Cerberus Jones

Cerberus Jones is the three-headed writing team made up of Chris Morphew, Rowan McAuley and David Harding.

Chris Morphew is *The Gateway's* main story architect. His job is to weave the team's ideas together into awesome, page-turning story outlines. Chris's experience writing adventures for *Zac Power* and heart-stopping twists for *The Phoenix Files* makes him the perfect man for the job!

Rowan McAuley is the team's chief writer. Her role is to expand Chris's outlines into fully-fledged novels, building the excitement and fleshing out the characters. Before joining Cerberus Jones, Rowan wrote some of the most memorable stories and characters in the best-selling *Go Girl!* series.

David Harding's job is editing and continuity. After Chris and Rowan have done their part, David arrives to iron out all the kinks. With his superior knack for spotting issues and coming up with solutions, David is the polish that makes *The Gateway* series shine! He is also the man behind *Robert Irwin's Dinosaur Hunter* series, as well as several *RSPCA Animal Tales* titles.

THE GATEWAY

THE FOUR-FINGERED MAN
Cerberus Jones

THE WARRIORS OF BRIN-HASK
Cerberus Jones

FOUR GREAT ADVENTURES

THE MIDNIGHT MERCENARY
Cerberus Jones

THE ANCIENT STARSHIP
Cerberus Jones